W9-DAP-741

Restless Earth

VOLCANOES AND EARTHQUAKES

Terry Jennings

Thameside Press

Distributed in the United States by
Smart Apple Media
1980 Lookout Drive
North Mankato, MN 56003

Text copyright © Terry Jennings

Editor: Julie Hill
Designers: Steve Wilson, Maria D'Orsi
Illustrator: Graham Rosewarne
Picture researcher: Diana Morris
Consultant: Stephen Watts

ISBN 1-931983-21-6

Library of Congress Control Number 2002 141363

Printed by Sino Publishing House Ltd, Hong Kong

Photographic credits

Axiom: 27b Jim Holmes. **Bruce Coleman Ltd:** 17b John Murray. **Eye Ubiquitous:** 22t
James Mollison. **Gamma:** back cover & 5t V. Shone. **GSF:** 21t. **Sonia Halliday Photographs:**
26. **Frank Lane Picture Agency:** 13b S. McCutchen. **Natural History Museum:** 27t. **Planet
Earth**: 4 A. & M. Magiani, 19b Chris Huxley. **G. R. Roberts:** 22, 25b. **Science Photo Library:**
front cover Explorer/Krafft, 5b Simon Fraser, 8 Martin Bond, 11b Peter Menzell, 12 David Hardy,
17t Ross Ressmeyer, 18 John Mead, 19t Peter Menzell, 21b NASA, 29t & b Ross Ressmeyer.
Frank Spooner Pictures: title page Gamma/Victoria Brynner, 9b, 11t Victoria Brynner.
Still Pictures: 16 Alain Compost, 25t B. & C. Alexander. **TRIP:** 15t Australian Picture
Library, 15b W. Jacobs, 24 M. Lee. **Zefa:** 23, 28 Lagerway.

Words in **bold** appear in the Glossary on pages 30 and 31.

Contents

The powerful earth

▲ *Popocatépetl Volcano in Mexico at sunrise. Quiet since 1928, this volcano began frequent eruptions in the mid 1990s.*

Volcanoes and earthquakes are some of the most powerful and destructive forces in nature. They can cause great damage and threaten the lives of people who live nearby. But **volcanoes** and **earthquakes** also help to shape our earth, forming mountains, valleys, and islands.

Our moving earth

The ground beneath our feet feels firm and hard. But really the surface of the earth is always moving—it just moves so slowly that we do not notice it. If we are not wearing shoes, the ground usually feels quite cool. But deep down some of the **rocks** are so hot that they have melted into liquid.

Erupting and shaking

Sometimes the melted rock from inside the earth pushes its way up to the surface through a crack or hole, called a volcano. We say that the volcano has **erupted**. When the melted rock cools, it forms a hill or mountain around the opening. In some places the moving surface of the earth shakes the ground. This causes an earthquake.

Shaping our earth

Erupting volcanoes and earthquake **tremors** can cause terrible damage. But they also change the landscape, helping to form mountains and valleys. Volcanoes build new rocks, and when these wear away, they often make **fertile** soil. Volcanoes can also help us to heat our homes and produce electricity.

The power of the earth

In this book we look at the causes of earthquakes and volcanic eruptions. We see how they change the earth and cause damage. We also discover how the great power in the moving surface of the earth can sometimes be used by people.

▲ *This earthquake in 1988 in the small country of Armenia caused great damage and many deaths.*

▼ *This fault line is in Iceland. Most earthquakes happen where land moves at a fault line.*

Beneath the surface

From a spacecraft the earth looks like a giant ball or sphere. But really the earth is like a huge onion, made up of layers. The layers of an onion are very similar, but the layers of the earth are very different from each other.

Fire down below

The outer layer of the earth—the one we stand on—is a thin layer of solid rock. This is called the earth's **crust**. Underneath the crust is a very thick layer of hot rocks, called the **mantle**. Parts of the mantle are so hot that the rocks have melted and flow like sticky tar.

The **core** in the middle of the earth is hotter still. It is made up of two parts. The outer core is made of hot, liquid iron, while the inner core is a hot ball of solid iron and nickel.

Inner core

Outer core

Mantle

Crust

◄ *The earth is made up of several layers of rock. The layer of rock that we live on is called the crust.*

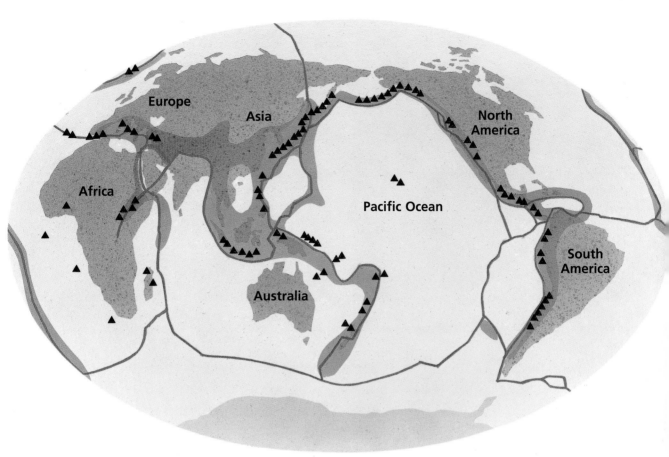

Plate boundaries
Earthquake zones
▲ Active volcanoes

▲ *The earth's crust is made up of huge pieces of rock, called plates. Most earthquakes and volcanoes are where the plates meet.*

Moving plates

The earth's crust is not just one huge skin of rock. It is made up of at least 20 pieces, called **plates**. These float on the molten rocks of the mantle. The plates are slowly pushed and pulled at about the speed at which our fingernails grow. As the plates bump into each other, they buckle at the edges and push up **folds** of the earth's crust. When the folds are small, they produce hills. When they are very large, they can go on to form huge mountain ranges, like the Alps in Europe, the Andes in South America, the Himalayas in Asia, and the Rocky Mountains in North America.

Most volcanoes are found where two or more of the earth's plates crash together or break apart. Most earthquakes also happen in these areas.

On shaky ground

▲ *These layers of rock have been folded by moving plates at the **San Andreas fault** on the west coast.*

Most rocks are hard and strong, but they still bend and fold to form hills and mountains. Rocks will also break. A rock is like the branch of a tree that will bend only so far until it snaps.

Sticking plates

The worst earthquakes happen where the earth's plates meet. The plates are always moving and usually slide past each other. But sometimes the edges of the plates stick together and cannot move. This puts pressure on the rocks until they bend. The rocks may also split, forming a crack called a **fault**.

Shocks and tremors

Pressure builds up as the plates push against each other. Suddenly they slip past each other as the pressure is released. The land above shakes violently. These sudden movements of the earth's crust are called shocks or tremors.

An earthquake is similar to what happens when a drawer sticks. You have to pull the drawer harder and harder to release it. Suddenly it gives way, and may come right out in your hand.

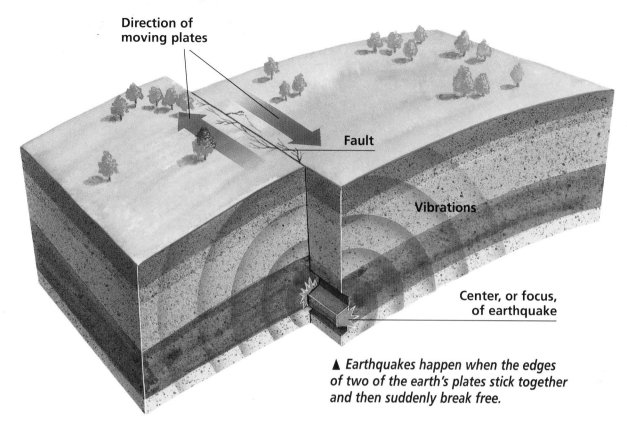

Direction of moving plates

Fault

Vibrations

Center, or focus, of earthquake

▲ *Earthquakes happen when the edges of two of the earth's plates stick together and then suddenly break free.*

Everyday earthquakes

Every day there are about 3,000 earthquakes. Most of them are so small that no one even notices them. About once a week there is an earthquake large enough to cause some damage. Every few months there is an earthquake so severe that it makes the ground shake violently. As the result of a serious earthquake in a city, roads may break up, bridges and buildings may collapse, and many people may be killed or injured.

► *This is what happened to a bridge after a serious earthquake in the Indian state of Uttar Pradesh on October 20, 1991.*

Earthquake zones

There are earthquake zones around the world, where most earthquakes happen.

Joints and faults

Most of the joints between the earth's plates are under the oceans and seas. But along the western side of the United States, one of these joints is on land. It is called the San Andreas fault. This huge crack in the rocks runs for nearly 600 miles along the coast of California. It passes near the cities of San Francisco and Los Angeles. Often there are mild earthquakes along the San Andreas fault. Sometimes there are severe earthquakes. An earthquake in San Francisco in 1989 killed 67 people, and another near Los Angeles in 1994 killed 61 people. Both earthquakes caused great damage.

More earthquake zones

Another earthquake zone runs through the Mediterranean Sea and across Southern Asia. A larger one goes around the Pacific Ocean from New Zealand up to Japan.

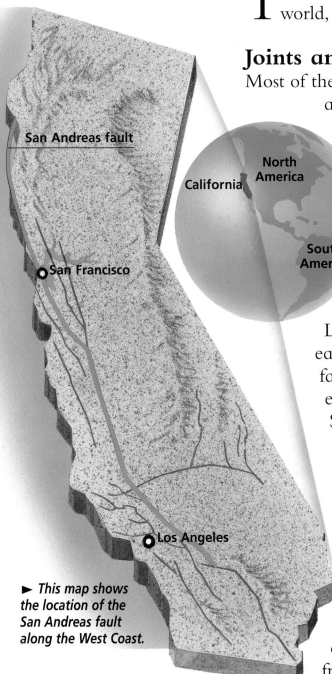

San Andreas fault

San Francisco

Los Angeles

North America

California

South America

► *This map shows the location of the San Andreas fault along the West Coast.*

It then runs down the western coast of North and South America (see map on page 7). Earthquakes can happen outside these zones, but they are usually mild.

Earthquake damage

Most earthquakes can only be recorded with scientific instruments. People living near the earthquake notice a slight shaking of the ground as if a truck is going past. Stronger earthquakes make tree leaves shake and church bells ring. A much bigger earthquake makes chimneys and trees fall down. The worst earthquakes break up roads and railroads. Buildings crack and fall down. Whole towns may be destroyed, and many people may be killed or injured.

▲ *This road was split down the middle by the earthquake near Los Angeles in 1994. Bridges and high rises also collapsed.*

▼ *Earthquake damage, San Francisco, 1989. These buildings, made with timber frames, toppled over easily during the earthquake.*

Walls of water

Tsunamis are long, high sea waves. They are often called tidal waves, even though they have nothing to do with tides. Most **tsunamis** are caused by earthquakes under the ocean. Underwater earthquakes are most common in the Pacific Ocean. A system has been set up there to warn people when tsunamis are likely to happen.

Epicenters

The **vibrations** from an earthquake are most violent near the fault that caused it. The place on the earth's surface above where an earthquake happens is called its **epicenter**. The vibrations spread out from the epicenter of the earthquake like the ripples made when you throw a stone into a pond.

High-speed waves

When an earthquake happens under the ocean, the vibrations also spread out in waves like the ripples on a pond. In the open ocean, the waves may be only a yard or so high. But tsunamis travel great distances very fast. They can reach speeds of more than 500 miles per hour. This is faster than many jet planes.

As a tsunami reaches shallow water, it slows down and grows to be enormous, reaching heights of 275 feet and sometimes more.

▲ *A painting of a tsunami. These huge walls of water are caused by underwater earthquakes and can reach heights of 275 feet.*

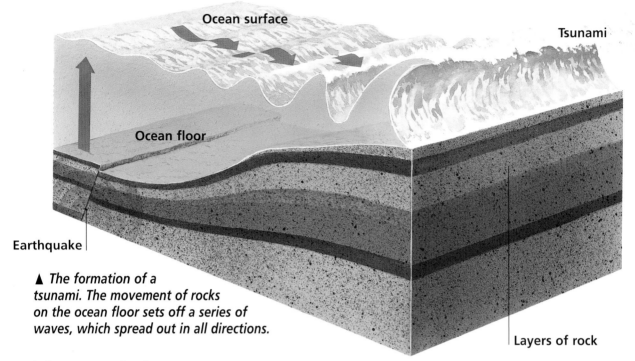

▲ The formation of a tsunami. The movement of rocks on the ocean floor sets off a series of waves, which spread out in all directions.

Ocean surface

Tsunami

Ocean floor

Earthquake

Layers of rock

Tsunami damage

Tsunamis can cause flooding, death, and destruction. The highest tsunami ever recorded was off the coast of Japan in April 1771. It reached a height of 278 feet.

A few tsunamis are caused when volcanoes under the ocean erupt. When the volcano erupted on the island of Krakatoa in 1883, it made the loudest noise ever recorded. People in Australia, about 3,000 miles away, heard the eruption. The land shook so violently that it caused nine huge tsunamis.

▼ This damage to the port of Seward in Alaska was caused by a huge tsunami.

Fiery volcanoes

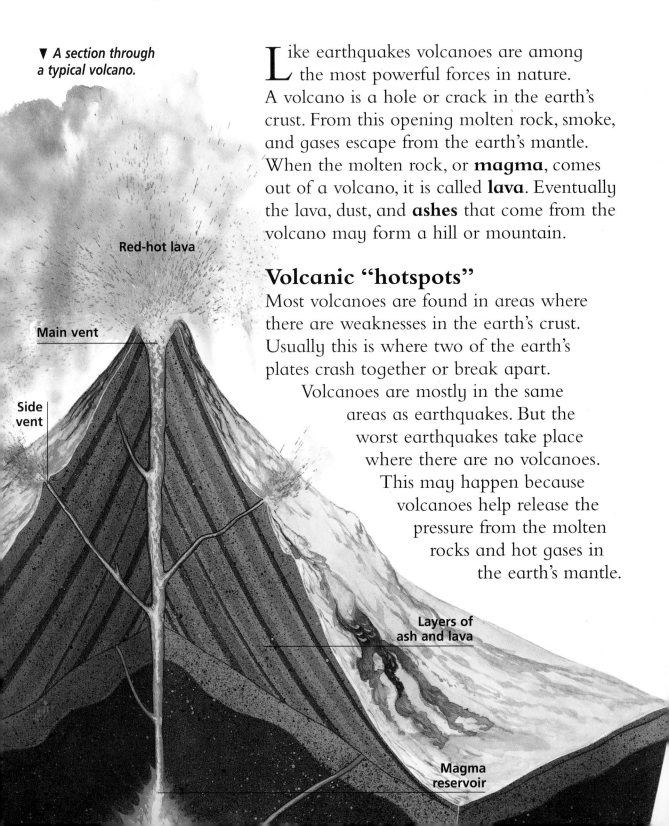

▼ *A section through a typical volcano.*

Red-hot lava

Main vent

Side vent

Layers of ash and lava

Magma reservoir

Like earthquakes volcanoes are among the most powerful forces in nature. A volcano is a hole or crack in the earth's crust. From this opening molten rock, smoke, and gases escape from the earth's mantle. When the molten rock, or **magma**, comes out of a volcano, it is called **lava**. Eventually the lava, dust, and **ashes** that come from the volcano may form a hill or mountain.

Volcanic "hotspots"

Most volcanoes are found in areas where there are weaknesses in the earth's crust. Usually this is where two of the earth's plates crash together or break apart.

Volcanoes are mostly in the same areas as earthquakes. But the worst earthquakes take place where there are no volcanoes. This may happen because volcanoes help release the pressure from the molten rocks and hot gases in the earth's mantle.

◄ The crater of the erupting Mount Ngauruhoe Volcano in New Zealand.

Around the top of the vent is a hollow, called the mouth or **crater** of the volcano.

Magma reaches the surface through the crater. In time other openings may appear in the sides of the volcano, and lava may burst out of these openings to produce extra lava flows. Rivers of lava can flow at speeds of 62 miles per hour.

Two thirds of the world's **active** volcanoes are found around the edge of the Pacific Ocean.

Inside a volcano

Where the earth's crust is weak or thin, magma rises from the mantle and forms large pools. These pools are called **magma reservoirs**.

The magma presses against the surrounding rock. When the magma finds a weak spot in the rock, it forces its way up. If the magma bursts through the earth's surface, a volcano is formed.

Magma flows

The magma flows up through a wide passage called a **vent**. Some vents are over 18 miles deep.

► This smoking lava from the Kalapana Volcano in Hawaii flows down the street like a river of fire.

Erupting volcanoes

Erupting volcanoes shoot out gases and lava. The lava may be red-hot or even white-hot. While it is still in the air, some of the lava cools to form ashes, dust, and lumps of rock.

Volcanic bombs

Some volcanoes erupt very violently. Red- or white-hot lava is blasted into the air, and some of it hardens into huge lumps of rock as it falls. These rocks are called **volcanic bombs**. Some of them weigh up to two tons and are thrown out over the surrounding land.

▼ *Volcanic bombs exploding out of Anak Krakatoa in Indonesia.*

◄ *People were buried alive in the deep ash that covered Pompeii after the eruption in* A.D. *79.*

The two towns stayed buried until the 18th century when people began to clear away the ash that had covered Pompeii. You can now walk around the streets of Pompeii and see it as it was on the day Vesuvius erupted in A.D. 79.

Rivers of mud

Volcanoes always produce large amounts of steam. When the steam cools, there is often a rainstorm. The rainwater mixes with the volcanic ash to form a muddy river, as happened at Herculaneum. Rivers of mud cause a lot of damage, and some of the gases given off are poisonous.

Eruptions in history

Mount Vesuvius is a volcano in southern Italy. Its most violent eruption was in A.D. 79. The top of the mountain was blown off, and two Roman towns, Pompeii and Herculaneum, were destroyed. Pompeii was buried in ash about twenty feet deep, and thousands of people were killed. After the eruption, Herculaneum was covered with streams of hot mud, when rain mixed with volcanic ash to form a muddy river.

▼ *The Giant's Causeway in Northern Ireland was formed from columns of hardened lava.*

Shapes of volcanoes

Not all volcanoes are high mountains. Some volcanoes are little more than a large hole or crack in the ground. Usually the lava from the volcano hardens quickly and piles up slowly. The hill around the vent of a volcano is called a **cone**. There are three main kinds of cones: **cinder cones**, **shield cones**, and **composite cones**.

Cinder cones

Some volcanoes erupt very violently. When the burning underground gases reach the surface, they rush out from the crater at the top of the cone.

◄ *Mount Haleakala in Hawaii is an example of a cinder cone.*

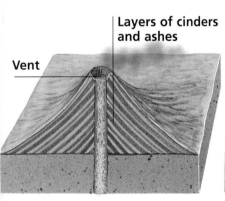

Vent | Layers of cinders and ashes

▲ *A section through a cinder cone.*

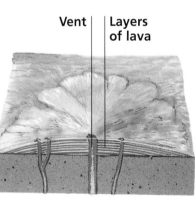

Vent | Layers of lava

▲ *A section through a shield cone.*

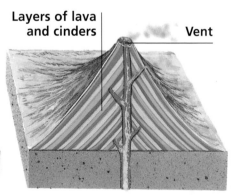

Layers of lava and cinders | Vent

▲ *A section through a composite cone.*

Hot ashes and **cinders** are forced high into the air, and volcanic bombs drop on the surrounding land. Such a violent eruption builds up a steep cone of ashes and cinders. Cinder cones are usually not more than about 1,000 feet high.

Shield cones

Some volcanoes erupt quietly. If the lava is fairly liquid, it spreads out around the crater of the volcano before it hardens. The lava forms a gently sloping volcano called a shield volcano.

▲ *Kilauea Volcano in Hawaii is an example of a shield volcano.*

Composite cones

Composite cones are made by volcanoes that sometimes erupt quietly and sometimes erupt very violently, throwing out cinders, ashes, and burning gases. The cones are called composite cones, because they are made of layers of different kinds of materials, like a layered cake. Composite cone volcanoes have steep sides and are often very high.

▼ *Cotopaxi in Ecuador, South America, is an example of a composite cone.*

Undersea volcanoes

There are many volcanoes on land, but there are even more volcanoes under the ocean. Volcanoes that erupt under the ocean are called **submarine volcanoes**. Sometimes when a submarine volcano erupts, a new island may form.

Surtsey: a new island

In November 1963, a fishing boat was sailing about 20 miles off the coast of Iceland. Suddenly the crew smelled burning, and a few moments later they saw a column of smoke rising from the ocean. They thought a ship was on fire, so they sailed toward the smoke.

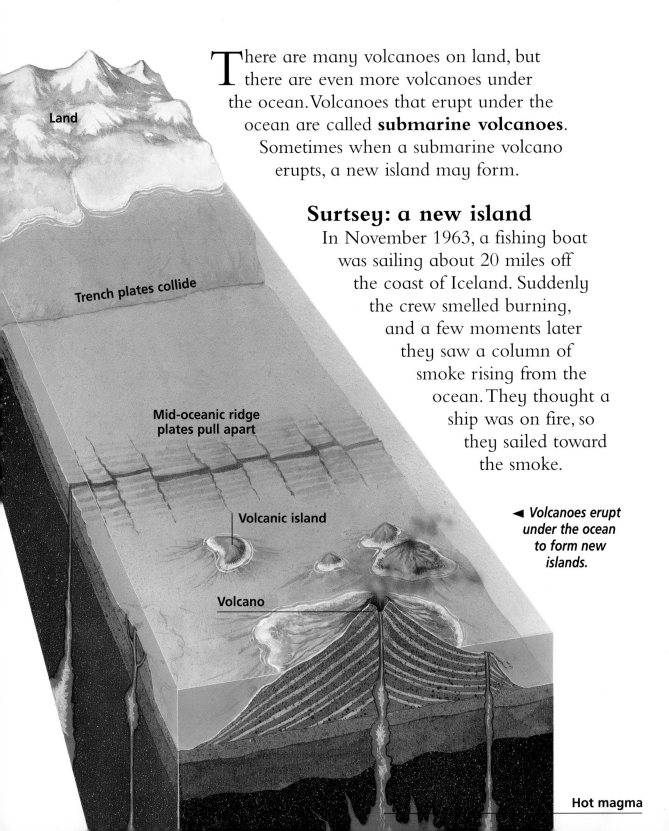

Land

Trench plates collide

Mid-oceanic ridge plates pull apart

Volcanic island

Volcano

◄ *Volcanoes erupt under the ocean to form new islands.*

Hot magma

As they drew closer, they realized that the smoke was pouring from a volcano beneath the ocean. The fishermen reported what they had seen, and scientists were able to watch a new island being formed. The volcano went on erupting, and in three months the island was about half a mile long. The island was named Surtsey, after Sutur, the Icelandic god of fire.

▲ *The volcanic eruption that formed the island of Surtsey off the coast of Iceland.*

The Hawaiian Islands

The Hawaiian Islands are a group of more than 100 islands in the Pacific Ocean. They were all formed by submarine volcanoes. One of the islands, Hawaii, is the top of a mountain more than 30,000 feets high. This is higher than Mount Everest, which is 29,028 feet high. Hawaii is made up of several volcanoes. One of them, Mauna Loa, is the largest active volcano in the world.

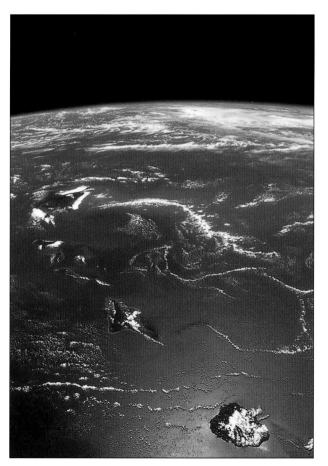

◄ *The Hawaiian volcanic islands, seen from a spacecraft. There are more than 100 islands in the group, but people live on only 14 of them.*

Dormant and extinct volcanoes

When gases and lava come out of a volcano, we say the volcano is erupting. A few volcanoes erupt all the time. Most volcanoes erupt only every now and then. A volcano that erupts is called active. There are about 1,300 active volcanoes in the world. Other volcanoes have not erupted for a very long time. These are called **dormant** or **extinct** volcanoes.

Dead volcanoes

Some volcanoes have not erupted for many thousands of years. There are no written records telling us when they last erupted. These volcanoes are called extinct.

▲ Mount Kilimanjaro in Tanzania is one of the world's largest extinct volcanoes.

◄ This volcano in New Zealand was active about 9,000 years ago. People now live and work around the crater.

Aconcagua in Argentina, South America, is the highest extinct volcano in the world. It is 22,835 feet high. Some other extinct volcanoes include Mount Taranaki in New Zealand, Kilimanjaro in Tanzania, and Mount Shasta in California.

Ngorongoro Crater

There is a huge extinct volcano in northern Tanzania called the Ngorongoro Crater. It measures more than 12 miles across. The floor of the crater is covered with dry, grassy plains, which are home

▲ *Wildebeests and zebras roaming the grassy plains of the Ngorongoro Crater in Tanzania. It is one of the largest craters in the world.*

to more than 30,000 wild animals, including lions, leopards, elephants, and wildebeests.

Sleeping volcanoes

Some volcanoes are called dormant, or sleeping. It is very difficult to say whether a volcano is dormant or extinct. Everyone thought that Eldfell Volcano on the island of Heimaey, near Iceland, was extinct. But in 1973 it erupted violently and destroyed about 300 buildings.

Geysers and hot springs

In many areas where there are volcanoes, there are also **geysers** and **hot springs**. A geyser is a natural spring that shoots columns of steam and hot water high into the air. Hot springs are similar to geysers, but the hot water only trickles from them.

Jets of steam

Geysers are found in volcanic areas where water can seep down through the ground. The water collects underground, where it is heated by hot rocks.

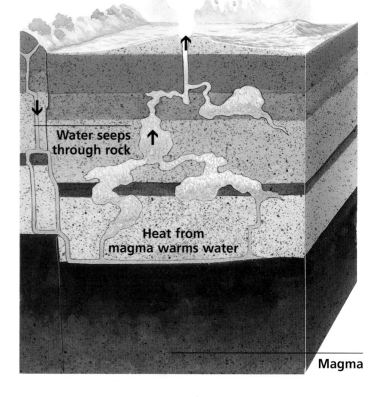

Geyser erupts

Water seeps through rock

Heat from magma warms water

Magma

▲ *Section through a geyser. Geysers occur where magma, or molten rock, lies near the earth's surface.*

◀ *Old Faithful Geyser in Wyoming. For hundreds of years this geyser has been erupting every hour.*

► *This swimming pool in Iceland is called the Blue Lagoon. Its waters are warm because they come from the geothermal power plant behind.*

Finally it turns into high-pressure steam and spurts out of the ground as a geyser. When enough water has seeped back through the ground, it is heated up again until another jet of steam and hot water is thrown into the air.

In some places the hot water becomes mixed with soil. It is then forced out of the ground as a **mud volcano**.

Useful geysers

Geysers attract lots of tourists. They also have other uses. In Iceland the water from hot springs is used to heat houses, apartments, and swimming pools. It is also used to heat greenhouses so that tomatoes, bananas, and other fruits can be grown. In several countries, such as Iceland, New Zealand, and parts of the United States, the water from hot springs is used to produce **geothermal energy**. Pipes take the hot water to a power plant, where it is used to make steam. Steam turns the **generators** that produce electricity.

► *A geothermal power plant near Rotorua in New Zealand. Rotorua is famous throughout the world for its hot springs and geysers.*

Useful volcanoes

▲ *Vineyards on the slopes of Mount Etna in Sicily, Italy. Its fertile slopes are good for growing crops.*

Although they are dangerous and can cause much damage, volcanoes can also be useful. They can be used for heating and to produce electricity. They also change the shape of the landscape, forming hills, mountains, and islands, and can produce fertile soils and valuable substances.

Fertile soils

Many people live on the slopes of volcanoes or in the valleys below. The soil on volcanic slopes is very fertile and good for growing crops. There are orchards and vineyards on the slopes of both Mount Vesuvius and Mount Etna in Italy.

Hardened lava

Solid lava is sometimes used to build houses and for making roads. Pumice stone is a very light rock formed from lava. It is used for rubbing away hard skin.

Valuable substances

Diamonds are used in jewelry and for cutting up rocks. Diamonds come from beneath the surface of the earth and are pushed up to the surface by volcanic eruptions.

▲ *This diamond has been pushed up to the surface by a volcanic eruption. Next to it is one that has been cut and polished.*

They can only be produced under the enormous pressures and high **temperatures** that exist beneath the earth's mantle.

The chemical called sulphur is found near some volcanoes. It is used for making rubber, gunpowder, dyes, fertilizers, and some ointments and medicines.

Famous volcanoes

Many tourists visit famous volcanoes such as Vesuvius, Stromboli, and Mount Etna in Italy and Fujiyama in Japan. The upper slopes of Mount Etna are even used for skiing in winter. Fujiyama is a holy site for Japanese people. Many thousands climb it every year.

▼ *People climb the extinct volcano Fujiyama in Japan every July and August. They go to watch the sun rise on the summit.*

Science at work

Scientists are trying to find out how to predict volcanic eruptions and earthquakes. They are also trying to stop earthquakes from happening.

Preventing earthquakes

An earthquake can sometimes be stopped by pumping water into rocks so that the edges of the jammed plates slip past each other. A small underground explosion can also make the plates move before too much pressure builds up.

Reducing damage

It is important to try to reduce earthquake damage. Nowadays in earthquake zones new buildings are built only on solid rock to hold them firm. They have a framework of strong steel that bends in an earthquake but will not collapse. Roofs are covered with rubber or plastic pads instead of tiles to reduce damage. Streets are wide, so that buildings will not block them if they fall.

◄ *This building in Tokyo, Japan, has been built with steel frames that will bend during an earthquake and so reduce damage.*

Predicting eruptions

People cannot keep a volcano from erupting, but it helps to know when an eruption is likely, so that people can be moved to safety.

Before a volcano erupts, the earth's crust shakes, and the volcano may swell up. The surrounding rocks and gases coming from the volcano may also change. All these things can be measured. Satellites **orbiting** the earth can also measure changes in the heat coming from the volcano.

▲ *These scientists are measuring the changes that take place when a volcano erupts.*

Stopping lava flows

Once a volcano is erupting, the lava can sometimes be made to flow away from a town or village. A large hole is dug in front of the stream of lava. The lava then fills up the hole before it flows on, giving people more time to escape. But in most cases nothing can be done. In the end the lava usually stops itself by cooling and becoming solid rock. This acts as a plug and stops the volcano from erupting.

▼ *A lava flow from Mount Etna in Italy during the eruption of the volcano in 1992.*

Glossary

active A volcano that erupts from time to time.

ash Fine particles of volcanic lava.

cinder A small piece of partlyburned material.

cinder cone A low volcano with a steep cone of ashes and cinders. Cinder cone volcanoes usually erupt violently.

composite cone A tall, cone-shaped volcano built up by many eruptions. It is made of layers of lava and layers of ashes and cinders.

cone The hill or mountain formed by a volcano.

core The center of the earth. The inner part of the core is probably a ball of very hot, solid metal. The outer part of the core is made of metal that is so hot that it has melted and is partly liquid.

crater The bowl-shaped hole at the top of a volcano.

crust The earth's outer layer of rock on which we live.

dormant Resting or inactive; not erupting.

earthquake A violent shaking of the ground caused by the earth's plates moving.

epicenter The point on the earth's crust that lies immediately above the center of an earthquake.

erupt The bursting out of magma from a weak spot in the earth's crust.

extinct No longer active.

fault A large crack or break in a series of rocks. The rocks on one or both sides of the fault may slip up or down.

fertile Land that is fertile has rich soil and produces good crops.

fold The bending of rocks caused by movements of the earth's surface.

generator A machine, sometimes called a dynamo, which produces electricity when it is turned.

geothermal energy Energy that is produced using the steam from water heated by the molten rocks beneath the surface of the earth.

geyser A hot spring that throws a jet of hot water and steam into the air from time to time.

hot spring A stream of hot water coming from the ground.

lava The hot, liquid (molten) rock that comes out of a volcano.

magma The molten rock found in the earth's mantle, just below the crust.

magma reservoir A large pool of magma beneath the surface of the earth.

mantle The layer of rock below the earth's crust and above the core. The mantle is thought to be so hot that some of the rocks have melted and are a sticky liquid.

mud volcano A mound of mud with a crater at the top. It is formed from hot water that has mixed with soil.

orbit The action of one object moving around another. The earth orbits the sun, and a satellite orbits the earth.

plates The sections of the earth's crust. The slow, steady movements of the plates cause changes in the earth's surface.

rock The solid part of the earth's crust beneath the soil.

San Andreas fault A huge crack in the earth's crust that runs along much of the western coast of the United States. Many earthquakes happen here.

shield cone A gently sloping volcano, formed by runny lava that has spread out around the crater of a volcano.

submarine volcano A volcano on the ocean bed.

temperature The degree of how hot or cold something is.

tremor A shaking or vibration of the ground caused by an earthquake.

tsunami A large ocean wave, usually caused by an earthquake on the ocean bed.

vent The opening in a volcano from which lava, gases, ashes, and cinders erupt.

vibration The action of moving quickly back and forth or up and down (vibrating).

volcanic bomb A lump of lava thrown out by a volcano. It is thrown out in liquid form, but while it is in the air, it turns solid.

volcano A hole or tear in the earth's crust from which molten rock (lava) flows.

Index